BRAMBLE and COULTOON'S JOURNEY

from ISLAY *(pronounced EYE-LA)* to SOUTH UIST a...

OUTWARD

RETURN

South Uist

4.

5.

1. **Coultoon**
2. **Port Askaig**
3. **Oban**
4. **Camp site**
5. **Prince's Cave**

Tiree

Coll

Colonsay

Iona

Mull

Islay

1.

2.

Jura

3.

Mainland

Published by AILSAPRESS 2009

Port Charlotte Isle of Islay PA48 7TS

www.ailsapress.com

ISBN 978-0-9555656-2-5

Also by Catherine Wilson and Ruth MacLean "The Tail of Ailsa" (2007)

FSC

Mixed Sources

Product group from well-managed
forests and other controlled sources

Cert no. TT-COC-002366
www.fsc.org
© 1996 Forest Stewardship Council

Printed and bound in Great Britain by

M & A Thomson Litho Ltd., East Kilbride, Scotland

This book is dedicated to Ben and Sean,
who were the first to meet Bramble and Coultoon.

Coultoon was born on the moss at Coultoon, which is why he was called Coultoon. Bramble was also born on the moss at Coultoon but he couldn't have the same name so he was called Bramble. Coultoon is on the island of Islay. They make whisky on Islay and there are lots of sheep.

In the picture, you can see the farm at Coultoon, with the two ponies and the sheep. You can also see the Paps of Jura beneath the rising sun.

One day while they were grazing, Bramble said to Coultoon in between munches, "I wonder if anything ever happens on the other side of Jura."
And Coultoon said, "I know. I've got a tent and we can take the tent for shelter and we can go and explore."

So they took a bag of Islay peat, a kettle and their tent, and they trotted off towards Jura with Coultoon leading the way and Bramble eagerly in pursuit. The peat was for a fire. The kettle was for making tea.

But when they got to the other side of Islay, they found the sea between Islay and Jura. And because they did not know how to swim, they decided to take the ferry to cross the sea. Though that was only part of the reason. The other reason was that Bramble did not want to get their peat wet. So Coultoon jumped on to the ferry and Bramble came soon afterwards.

They had a picnic of some hay and some chocolate on board the ferry. The other passengers were amazed. They had never seen two ponies travel across the sea before. At long last, they were told that the ferry was arriving at OBAN.

"Where is Oban?" Coultoon asked the man with binoculars.

"Is it on Jura?" asked Bramble.

"Dear me no! Oban is on the mainland. We just sailed past Jura," he said.

Bramble and Coultoon were rather sad.

"Oh dear, we didn't mean to come to Oban. We wanted to go to Jura."

Some passing gulls started to laugh. "Ka-ka-ka! They wanted to go to Jura, and they've come to Oban. Ka-ka-ka!" And the gulls went on shrieking until Bramble got very cross.

"Of course we wanted to come to Oban. We wanted to see what was on the other side of Jura. Come on, Coultoon. Let's get on another ferry and see what happens on the other side of Oban!"

It was a very rough crossing on the ferry. Coultoon's great-uncle, who had been a fisher pony, used to say:

> *'If you're down below decks in a gale,*
> *Your breakfast will up in a pail.'*

So Coultoon and Bramble stayed out on deck and they were not sick, just a little bit uncomfortable. At last some mountain tops appeared between the troughs of the waves. It was the island of South Uist.

"LAND-HO!" cried Bramble. "About time too," said Coultoon, who was truly not feeling very well.

Bramble and Coultoon trotted off with their peat, their kettle and their tent until they found a nice place to camp. It was on the side of a mountain. They put up their tent and before they went to bed, Bramble laid the peats in a circle so they could make a fire the next day. Coultoon filled up the kettle with water and put it on top of the peats.

"First up makes the tea!" said Bramble just before he closed his eyes. But Coultoon did not hear him because he was already sound asleep.

"Wake up Bramble!" said Coultoon.

"I am awake, Coultoon. I was thinking, shall we go to the other side of the mountain today?"

"Good idea, Bramble. Let's have tea first."

Soon the kettle was on the boil and they made their morning tea. They each took turns to hold the kettle in their mouth so the other could drink the tea. And in case you're wondering how they made the fire, this is what they did. They struck their hooves against the stones until there were sparks and the sparks made the peat catch fire.

Bramble was surprised. He said, "Coultoon, there's a man over there cutting peat. Let's talk to him!"

Coultoon was shy. "You talk, Bramble," he said.

Bramble explained to the man that they came from Islay.

"Islay!" the peat man exclaimed. "I've heard of Islay. It's famous for whisky."

"Could you tell us, please, what happens on the other side of the mountain?"

"That's where you'll find the Prince's Cave!"

Bramble and Coultoon were excited. They wanted to find the Prince's Cave and the Prince too.

It was a very long way to the other side of the mountain. They went up and up and up and then they went down. It was very steep so they had to go very slowly or else they would fall. At last they got to the bottom. They stood by a waterfall and they looked up. They could see a dark hole in the edge of a cliff. It was the entrance to a cave. They were very curious and a little bit frightened.

Bramble said, "Shall we look inside the cave?"

"You go first, Bramble," said Coultoon. "You're the brave one!"

Coultoon was just about to follow Bramble when he heard someone behind him. He turned round and he saw a handsome man in a kilt and a bonnet. He forgot all about being shy.

"Are you the Prince?" he asked.

"I am honoured to meet you!" replied the stranger.

"Do you live here?" asked Coultoon.

"No, my country is far away," replied the Prince.

By this time, Bramble was also looking at the handsome stranger. "Our island is far away too," he said. "We've come a long way from home."

Prince Charlie *for that was the Prince's name* made the two ponies an offer. He said, "If you help me sail my ship, I will offer you to take you home."

Bramble and Coultoon were surprised to see a sailing ship in the bay below. It was anchored and it had red sails and tall masts.

"Quick, all aboard!" cried the Prince.

"What about our tent?!" exclaimed Bramble.

"Pack it!" said the Prince.

"And our kettle!" said Coultoon.

"Pack it too!" said the Prince.

The two ponies helped sail the ship. They held on to the ropes and took turns at the tiller. The Prince climbed the mast to look for the Paps of Jura. After two days and two nights, the Prince cried, "Look! The Paps of Jura! We must be near Islay now."

Soon they had brought the ship into Port Askaig. They all got off and went to the hotel for some refreshment. The ponies had a bucket of fresh water each, and the Prince had a good dram of ISLAY WHISKY.

"Hmm!" he said. "This is the spirit of life! Bring me a barrel! I shall sail happily now for France!"

Bramble and Coultoon returned to the moss at Coultoon. Sometimes, one or other of them would look up at the Paps of Jura and wonder.

"Do you remember when we travelled with our tent to the other side of Jura?"

"Yes, and we met Bonnie Prince Charlie!"

"I wonder if he got home alright."

"I expect he did. After all, there were lots of other Islay ponies who wanted to sail with a Prince."

"Yes, yum. I'm glad I'm back home."

"So am I. The grass is so green here, yum-yum."

THE END